Thomas Gets a Snowplow

A Random House PICTUREBACK® Book
Illustrated by Richard Courtney

Random House New York

Thomas the Tank Engine & Friends®

A BRITT ALLCROFT COMPANY PRODUCTION

Based on The Railway Series by The Reverend W Awdry. © 2004 Gullane (Thomas) LLC.
Thomas the Tank Engine & Friends and Thomas & Friends are trademarks of Gullane Entertainment Inc.
Thomas the Tank Engine & Friends is Reg. U.S. Pat. TM Off.

A HIT Entertainment Company

www.randomhouse.com/kids/thomas   www.thomasthetankengine.com
Library of Congress Control Number: 2004103703
ISBN 0-375-82783-8 Printed in the United States of America First Edition 20 19

Early one winter morning, Thomas rolled out of his shed to check the weather. It had snowed a little each day all week. It wasn't snowing just then, but the sky was gray and threatening.

"Looks like we're going to have to get out your snowplow soon, Thomas," said his driver.

Thomas was a Really Useful Engine, but he did not like wearing a snowplow. "No!" he said with a frown. "I'm fine just as I am. Besides, my branch line was clear yesterday. I don't *need* a snowplow. It's not even snowing!"

"But, Thomas," said his driver, "your snowplow would help you be Really Useful. Why don't you want to use it?"

"Snowplows look silly!" Thomas grumbled. "The other engines will laugh at me."

His driver looked up at the cloudy sky and back down at Thomas. "Well, it isn't snowing yet," he said. "Maybe you won't need your snowplow today after all. But you haven't used it since last winter, and we need to make sure it's still in working order. So you're going to have to try it on."

"All right," Thomas grumbled reluctantly.

When he saw the snowplow, Thomas felt like steaming away. He *really* didn't want to put it on, but he had agreed. So with a few turns of a screw and a few twists of a bolt, Thomas had a snowplow attached to his front.

"There now!" said his driver. "It fits perfectly."

Just then, James and Henry pulled out of the shed and saw Thomas.

"Ha! Look, Henry," said James. "Thomas is wearing a snowplow! It looks like a tin can!"

The two engines chuckled and chortled. "It's not even snowing! *I* wouldn't need a snowplow in this weather," Henry said. "I'm big enough to get through plenty of snow without one!"

Thomas blushed and looked down. "Please take it off," he whispered to his driver.

"All right," said his driver kindly. "But we may need to come back for it," he added, with another nervous glance at the sky.

When Thomas started out, there was some snow on the ground, but the tracks were clear. He didn't need a snowplow at all!

His first stop was at a small station by an inn. As Thomas was pulling up, it started snowing lightly. The innkeeper hurried out to unload supplies. "Mighty cold winter we're having, Thomas!" he said. "I'll need these extra blankets for my guests."

"Peep, peep!" And Thomas was off again.

Thomas' next stop was at the general store, where he had a large delivery to make. "Thank you, Thomas," said the owner of the store. "With this weather, I can *never* have enough snow shovels, hats, and mittens! My customers will be very happy."

Thomas smiled, peeped a farewell, and was on his way once more.

By the time Thomas made his last stop, it was snowing hard. The trip home was very difficult. The snow was piling up on the tracks, and it was hard to see. Thomas just went steadily on, concentrating on his warm shed and the other engines waiting for him at the end of the line.

See, Thomas thought, *I can do this* without *a silly snowplow.*

Finally, Thomas managed to get back to the shed. Percy, James, and Henry were talking about the snow. "I've never seen it snow so hard," said Percy.

Suddenly Sir Topham Hatt hurried in. "Toby is stuck on his branch line!" he said. "We need to go get him or he may be out in the snow all night. Henry, you're the biggest engine here, so you will have to do it."

"But it's snowing so hard, and it is so cold," said Henry.

Sir Topham Hatt gave Henry a stern look.

Henry quickly changed his mind and said, "But I am faster than Percy, James, or Thomas, *and* I'm big enough to get through this snow without a snowplow." So Sir Topham Hatt climbed aboard, and they were off.

Thomas' driver looked with concern at the swirling snowstorm. "I'm putting on your snowplow," he said. "I have a bad feeling about this snow."

So with a few turns of a screw and a few twists of a bolt, Thomas had his snowplow on again.

"Thank you, Thomas," said Toby. "I would've been out in the cold all night if it weren't for you and your snowplow. I wish a snowplow would fit over *my* cowcatcher!"

Sir Topham Hatt smiled and said, "Yes, Thomas, you are a Really Useful Engine, and today you are a hero as well."

Thomas beamed. For once he was happy to be wearing his snowplow...no one could see him blushing.

Thomas crept past Toby and switched onto the same track. He carefully backed up to Toby. His driver jumped down and hooked them together. "Now pull!" his driver called.

Thomas pulled. He pulled as hard as he could. Slowly but surely, Toby began to move. And slowly but surely, Thomas pulled Toby through the snowstorm.

Soon Thomas could tell that what looked like a mound of snow on the track ahead of him was actually Toby, buried deep.

"*Peep, peep!* Toby! I'm here to help you!" called Thomas.

Thomas thought about how the other engines had laughed at his snowplow. Then he thought about Toby having to stay out in the snow all night. "Sir, with my snowplow, I can do it!" Thomas said.

The snow was deep along the track, but that was no problem for Thomas' snowplow. It was still hard to see, but Thomas went slowly and carefully.

Just then, the engines saw a strange sight. It was hard to tell in
the thick snow, but it looked like Henry, backing up into the yard.

"I couldn't make it," Henry steamed as he came closer. "The track
was covered in snow. I almost got stuck. I could barely back out."